I0654318

Opening Nights

A Collection of Theater Stories

Bev Denor
Rick Gerroll
Kevin Hansen
Gary Retzak
Kerry A. Trask
Emily M. Trask
Brad Zimmermann

ISBN: 979-8-9912318-3-1
Library of Congress Number: 2024946347

Fresh Water Press LLC
PO Box 425
Two Rivers, WI 54220

freshwaterpressllc.com

Dedication

To the artists, writers, actors, musicians, and all creative spirits of the lakeshore. You enrich our communities.

Table of Contents

Foreward

Fresh Water Press began with an idea to enrich the literary landscape of the greater lakeshore area of northeastern Wisconsin. The idea grew from a writing circle, where Tracey Koach, Tara Huck, and Peggy Turnbull discovered a shared love of literature and agreed that untapped talent was readily available nearby. With a commitment to bringing quality books to the shelves, we developed a business plan with the hopes of discovering rich stories ready to be published.

During a conversation about the press with Bev Denor, our neighbor, and the owner of an independent bookstore, she shared that she had edited a collection of short stories some time ago. This serendipitous conversation led to her sharing *Opening Nights* with us, a manuscript that she recovered from her basement.

We quickly fell in love with the charm of this anthology of local writers celebrating amateur theater through short stories. It was an enthusiastic, unanimous decision to bring this beauty to fruition, a book twenty-plus years in the making.

Fresh Water Press is happy to put the spotlight on local authors presenting a show to savor! We hope you enjoy these stories as much as we do, and that they leave you entertained.

Tara Huck
Tracey Koach
Peggy Turnbull

Preface

Opening Nights began as a project to divert my friend and me from committing a crime. OK. Maybe not a crime, but at the very least we had planned quite a clandestine activity! What it was shall forever remain a secret. I believe that by this time both of us have forgotten just what it was that had us meeting once a month at "Kristina's" . . . what could it have been that brought us to hushed conversation over the Greek olive and goat cheese appetizer, and flourless chocolate cake with raspberry syrup for dessert? Well, looking back it seems that the mystery is now greater in the forgetting than in remembering.

One Tuesday, having tired of the endless assignments we gave each other that always resulted in no progress, no information, and less and less talk of the project, I arrived at the restaurant with a copy of *Coming Home to Door,* a collection of short stories set in and around Door County, Wisconsin, edited by Wisconsin Rapids writer and publisher, Casey Martin.

"We can do this," I announced. That was that. One frivolous intrigue set aside and replaced with a challenge both entertaining and attainable. Over shared crab cakes with red pepper sauce, we set the parameters for the stories. Each must be set in the lakeshore and take place on the opening night of a local theater production. Simple.

From there we invited writers, pitched the project, set deadlines and waited. Then we set new deadlines and waited some more. Finally, we threatened and then all the stories, wild, wonderful, and melodramatic came pouring in.

Those of you who dabble in theater as some of us do will recognize yourself, your friends and productions in which you have been involved. Those of you entertaining the thought of carrying a spear proudly across stage may . . . well, why not just grab a cup of Jamaican Blue and read on.

—*Bev Denor, 2004*

Acknowledgments

From Bev Denor's Original Manuscript

Special thanks go to Mary "Casey" Martin of Home Brew Press in Wisconsin Rapids for her encouragement and spirit, Kevin Hansen for his cover artwork, Chris Lochmann for hours of formatting, and to Gary Retzak for one day saying to me, "Hey, have you ever thought about writing a book?"

*

From the Fresh Water Press

Our heartfelt thanks go to Bev Denor, who brought *Opening Nights* to our attention and whose vision and hard work were the driving forces that brought the original manuscript into being. Thank you to the authors: Rick Gerroll, Kerry Trask, Kevin Hansen, Bev Denor, Emily M. Trask, Gary Retzak, and Brad Zimmerman. You entrusted us with work you wrote so long ago that you may have thought it would never see the light of a reading lamp again. We are honored to present *Opening Nights* as the Fresh Water Press's debut publication.

Thank you, too, to Michael Sheeks and Bill Fricke, for contributing back cover appreciations from your perspectives as members of the local theater community.

And to our spouses Michael, P.J., and Bob, we are grateful to each of you for sharing expertise, information, and a listening ear during the formative months of the Fresh Water Press.

Opening Night

by
Rick Gerroll

It started with the makeup
when I couldn't get it right;
Then wardrobe brought my shirt in
and the collar was too tight.

The shoes, they said, were perfect
but the left one pinched a lot;
Besides that, I was freezing
while the rest of them were hot.

My throat was feeling scratchy and,
I thought, a little hoarse;
I finally got the costume right
and had to pee, of course.

And after I had finished
and my hands were washed and wet
I found no one put the towels in
the damn dispenser yet.

I used a roll of paper
from the wheelchair toilet stall,
Wiped my hands and blew my nose,
then slipped and took a fall.

I heard a tear go up my back,
get worse as I arose,
Caught the bottom of the door
and snagged my pantyhose.

I had to run or die in there,
was evidently clear,
I saw I'd blown my makeup off
when looking in the mirror.

Then I heard "Five minutes, please,"
and had a heart attack
While racing down to wardrobe,
dress wide open in the back.

Duct taped up the gaping hole
while changing pantyhose;
Tried to keep my head still
as they remade up my nose.

"One minute, please." I heard her voice,
I flew to take my place.
The curtain up, my toe was caught,
I fell flat upon my face.

The audience erupted, joy
and laughs with their applause.
I hoped my bleeding nose would stop
while searching for some gauze.

My ankle felt a little weak.
I watched it warm and swell.
I didn't think it broken—
sometimes it's hard to tell.

I hobbled slowly to my feet,
a grimace with my smile,
Thinking to get through this show
was going to take some guile.

The other actors entered
and I knew things would be fine.
The dialogue began to flow
when I forgot my line.

I hesitated just a bit
in hopes the line would come.
My mind had drawn a total blank—
now weren't we having fun?

The other members in the cast
just glared in disbelief,
Like I was robbing them of jewels
and was a master thief.

I grabbed a line from nowhere
with which to save the day
and calmly, though with drama, said,
"I don't know what to say."

Pretty much downhill from there,
it really was a sight.
The critics made us close the show.
My debut opening night!

But it's OK, my new career
is going very well.
I'm working with the public
and they like me, I can tell.

It's not the same as show biz,
and I'm glad we had this chat.
And thank you for your order, say—
did you want fries with that?

The Intruder

by
Kerry A. Trask

Who's there!? What the hell is going on back here!?"
That's what I shouted at the top of my voice as I rushed backstage
and fumbled for the light switch. Once I could see, I conducted a
police-like search of the dressing rooms and storage closets until I
was satisfied not another human soul was in the place. In the end, the
mystery of what or who had caused the loud commotion still
remained a mystery.

We, that is the students and I, had been putting in a marathon
session to rehearse the remaining wrinkles and rough spots out of the
play we were doing. Time was running out and there still remained
far too many flaws, some metaphorically the size of bomb craters,
most of which appeared well beyond the ability of my student actors
to fix. In fact, our long and arduous rehearsal had done little more
than wear them out and make them supremely irritated, and near
midnight I was pretty much resigned to stoically accepting what
appeared doomed to become an inescapable disaster. But I didn't tell
them that. Instead, I used my remaining energy to give a rousing pep
talk that turned out to be one of the better acting performances of my
career.

I lied. Like a relapsed Nazi, I resorted to the theory that the
bigger the lies and the more times they were repeated, the more
likely they would be believed. I almost blushed at times, but what I
said seemed to diminish the glumness of the group and they didn't
even whine, not much at least, when I told them I wanted to run over
the whole thing one more time, straight through, at six o'clock the
next morning. It would be our last desperate whack at the thing
before opening night.

Quite frankly, I was relieved to see them go, and once the
front doors of Founders Hall had slammed and rattled shut and the
last of their headlights had disappeared over the Viebahn Street hill, I
returned to my office with good intentions of grading some essay

exams I'd neglected for far too long. I was tired but far too tense for sleep.

It was pleasantly cool and quiet in the building and the only sounds were those of the periodic flushing of the urinals in the men's room down the hall and the clicking on and off of the cooling system in the drinking fountain. The peacefulness felt wonderful. I fidgeted with the blue books for a minute or two, then picked up a rubber band, which I pulled between my fingers and shot a wad of paper out into the hall. Although I tried concentrating on the work at hand, my mind wandered and inevitably drifted back to the play.

We were doing *Our Town*. That hadn't been my idea—not on your life—and if it had been my shot to call, I'd have put it very far down on my list of possibilities. That wasn't because it was a bad play. It was quite good, in fact, but it had been put on for decades by virtually every high school, college and community theater group in the country. There were now hundreds, probably thousands, of women who could boast (and did) of having once acted the part of sweet, precocious Emily Webb, and just as many men who never tired of retelling their theatrical war stories about when they'd played the Stage Manager. It was to the point where clever new interpretations seemed unimaginable, and too many audience members knew the lines as well as the actors. There were no surprises left to be had.

The decision to do *Our Town* had been made by his eminence John Wesley Jarvis, or Professor John Wesley Jarvis, as he insisted on being addressed. He had been the longtime speech and theater instructor at UW-Manitowoc, a two year campus of the University of Wisconsin Colleges, located on the shore of mighty Lake Michigan just south of town. I'm almost certain Jarvis had picked it as an easy, almost sure way of selling enough tickets to fill most of the excruciatingly uncomfortable seats in what was a pitiful excuse for a college auditorium. Attendance had been down the past few years and the dean had told Jarvis he had better turn it around . . . so, because Manitowoc people were such sentimental suckers for the old familiar favorites, he must have assumed Thornton Wilder's small town classic would be a big hit.

Jarvis hadn't always had to resort to such strategies. When he'd first come to the college from the Twin Cities in the mid-1960s he'd set the lakeshore theater scene ablaze. He was a high-strung individual who often wandered the halls completely entranced in his own thoughts, only to abruptly erupt into a spontaneous soliloquy when greeted by a simple hello. An unusually charming, highly intelligent man with some very definite charismatic qualities, he had easily attracted droves of enamored admirers. Jarvis excited people and in those early days all his shows were sellouts evoking thunderous standing ovations. Furthermore, he miraculously managed to accomplish all that on the college's miserly budget, and in a theater that was embarrassingly inadequate.

He was a tight, tense, wiry man, of inexhaustible energy who kept himself in superb physical condition and wore his hair nearly as short as two-day-old whisker stubble. He looked and acted more like a Marine than a college professor, and it was that persona which ironically accounted for his unusual success as a teacher and theater director. Besides that, everything about him was expressive—his hands, his posture, his weather creased face, and especially his voice made even more richly resonant by the Lucky Strikes he smoked without ceasing.

Jarvis's personal and artistic powers had soon become almost legendary. Then suddenly, after many years and one particularly demanding semester, for no known or understood reason, they were gone. His creative fire and dramatic flare burned out leaving nothing but ashes, transforming him into a sullen, sarcastic curmudgeon of a man easily annoyed by students and listlessly indifferent toward his work. All that remained of his former self was his obsessive passion to control every aspect of the small theatrical empire he'd created through his long succession of triumphant conquests. Indeed, he'd become the very embodiment of what every teacher and artist lives in fear of becoming: someone who, without fault or intention, outlives the muse that has been his inspiration and source of meaning to be left empty and deprived of purpose and without hope of regeneration, and yet too stubborn and narcissistic to relinquish control and step aside.

Then, one morning this past October, the dean, arriving at work a little after dawn, discovered John Wesley Jarvis stone cold dead at his desk. His heart had stopped, and he'd died in an instant, slumped over the clutter of long-ignored work with a Lucky Strike still burning in his ashtray.

I was clearly a reactive hire hastily brought in to fill the void, young and naive and easygoing, originally from Copper Harbor in the Upper Peninsula, and overeager for steady work. I was picked from a short list of decidedly undistinguished candidates and hired by the dean to clean up the mess left behind by the late John Wesley Jarvis's untimely departure. By the time I came on, the semester was well under way and the *Our Town* production was in terrible shape. It had to be rebuilt from the ground up, which proved to be hard and thankless work. Besides, death had made Jarvis once again a revered figure, and students never hesitated to tell me that the great professor would not approve of what I was doing to his play. Sometimes, I even got the creepy feeling he was still around, somewhere behind the scenes, watching me from the shadows like some beast of prey slowly moving in for the kill.

That feeling had been particularly strong the night of the unexplained noise backstage. Immediately on entering the theater I caught the unmistakable smell of cigarette smoke in the air. None of the kids in the cast, nor any of the night janitors smoked, nevertheless, I soon inexplicably discovered in one of the dressing rooms two short, unfiltered cigarette butts stubbed out among some ashes at the bottom of an otherwise empty, dark blue Noxzema jar. And the jar was still warm. It was downright baffling, even a little spooky, but far too late to fret about just then.

The following morning our rehearsal went better than expected. Perhaps the fear of being on the brink of disaster had finally hit home. There's nothing quite like fear to focus one's attention. Throughout the day the suspense built and by early evening we had all come down with dry mouths and queasy stomachs. But my mildly amusing preshow speech helped convert some of that nervousness into productive energy, and once the curtain went up the kids quickly got into the groove. The audience, which was larger than we anticipated for a Thursday night, chuckled at the pedantic performance of Professor Willard, jeered a little when boozed up and morose Simon Stimson shouted at the ladies of the church choir, and then they broke into a roar when Julia Gibbs invited her husband Frank to "Come out and smell my heliotrope in the moonlight."

"Nice going, you're really breaking legs out there," I said to the cast upon making it through the first act.

The second act went every bit as well, and we were on an exhilarating roll by the time we were coming into the home stretch in the third. The last act evoked some powerful emotions. In it the young and endearing heroine, Emily Webb, dies in childbirth and then comes back to relive one day of her life. It is tear-jerking stuff and much of the action takes place in the town cemetery, where besides Emily, many other deceased residents of Grover's Corners gather to ponder the meaning of life and death. In the gloomy light, they sit almost lifelessly in two rows of straight-backed chairs.

The curtain rose. Everyone was in place and even the kid playing Joe Stoddard, the town undertaker, got his lines right for the first time ever. Then, from my position in the control room at the back of the theater, I observed an empty extra chair on stage. One of the stagehands must have screwed up, I thought. But nobody else seemed to pay it any attention. They were all mesmerized by Emily. While the audience leaned forward, captivated by the scene, I suddenly caught the distinct scent of cigarette smoke and wondered, in quiet irritation, who the hell might be smoking in the theater. But soon again all my attention was drawn back to Emily as she sobbed and declared, "I can't! I can't go on! It goes so fast! We don't have the time to look at one another."

While everyone's attention remained glued upon Emily, then bidding a sorrowful farewell to her butternut tree, hot baths, freshly ironed dresses, I noticed a thin, pale, nearly bald figure sitting in what had been that unexplained empty chair. As soon as my focus bore in upon him he slowly raised his head and glared directly into my eyes with a resentful and disapproving stare. I shuddered as a cold shock of terror surged through my entire being. "Sweet Jesus," I gasped, "It's John Wesley Jarvis!"

The entire audience remained completely absorbed in the heart-wrenching scene, some wiping tears from their cheeks. Then my attention momentarily shifted again to Emily as she asked, "Do any human beings realize life while they live it—every, every minute?" And when I looked back Jarvis was gone.

Later, I wondered if he'd ever really been there, or whether the ghostly apparition I thought I'd seen was simply the creation of my tired and anxious imagination. After everyone had left, leaving me completely alone once more, I walked across the stage in the quiet of the empty theater and there, beneath that mysterious extra chair, I discovered the burned out remains of a carelessly discarded Lucky Strike.

Fifteen years later . . .

John Wesley Jarvis's apparition was never seen or heard from again after that Thursday night. The narrator, on the other hand, after recovering from a mild nervous breakdown, went on to surpass Jarvis in both brilliance and popularity with his theater presentations. He thrived well beyond his own expectations. He earned tenure, got promoted, outlived the dean (who came down with his own severe and protracted case of professional burnout), and went on to become chancellor of the University of Wisconsin Colleges. Some powerful people in the state even encouraged him to run for governor. In the end, however, following his unanticipated and unexplained resignation, and then hastily leaving town with an unusually agile UW-Madison cheerleader, he died when the flight they were on crashed in the frozen wastelands of northern Greenland.

Although his earthly remains were recovered and interred in his beloved Upper Peninsula, there were, from time to time, rumors about his spirit returning to inhabit the quiet darkness of Founders Hall on opening nights.

Bad Decisions

by
Kevin Hansen

I have made my share of bad decisions in the past. Today I am going to realize my latest. Sometimes I wonder why I even get out of bed.

11:45 a.m. Here I sit on a barstool at Little Joe's Bar and Grill. A few chairs down sit a couple. Retired. She from the offices of Hamilton Manufacturing Company, he from building cranes at the Manitowoc Company. They were discussing the foul odor the alewives were sending in from the lakeshore. She feels it had been worse in years past. He thinks it hasn't. They are regulars here and their conversations always go the same. Whatever she says, he disagrees. Behind the bar Little Joe is washing up some glasses while Dolores is busy at the grill and working the deep fryer. I come to this place often. I had ordered a liver and bacon sandwich and a coke. This is my place to think. Small conversation when I need it, and when I just want to sit, people let me do just that.

I have a lot to think about. As I sip my coke and stare at the gold and silver foiled picture of Little Joe with Grubby the Monkey, I just can't come to terms with what I had done just eight weeks ago. I had seen a lot of community theater. At every show I kept thinking I could do that, I could get up on stage and act out a part and I bet I'd be good at it, too. This kind of talk in my head during a performance went on for many years. And now here I am, just hours away from being someone the audience would be watching. I had made a very bad decision.

"Order up!" yells Dolores to Joe. Moments later, "A liver and bacon sandwich $3.75, thank you much." This will be my last meal before tonight. I am eating now because I know my stomach will not be able to keep anything down later. I am not even sure it can keep this down now, but I figure by the time I get on stage any food I eat at lunch will have absolutely no chance of coming up between the hours of 8 and 10 p.m.. I hope I'm right. I take a bite of the burger. This meal will not go down easy.

What if I forget something? What if I don't hear my cue? What if I forget to pull up my zipper? These questions keep rolling over and over in my head. Rehearsals had gone fine. In fact, better than fine, they were great. I knew what I was saying by the third rehearsal. I was confident of where to stand. I even looked like I was listening to the other characters as they spoke. My God, I was acting! This was what I dreamt of doing all those dark evenings in row P of the Capitol Civic Centre. When a show was bad I would think, I could have done that part better. And when a show was good, I dreamt of how wonderful it would be to have been a part of that. Now I just want to throw up.

Get a grip, OK, calm down. Everything will be OK, just take a deep breath and try to think of something else. Like the review in tomorrow's paper. "Show, Great Success, except for one newcomer to the community theater stage." Oh, I can just read it now. Stop it. I will be great. I'm going to be part of a great show and I'm going to help make it great. It's nice to know all those success seminars at work are finally coming in handy. All I have to do is remain positive and remember what it is I have to do on stage tonight.

9:45 p.m. OH MY GOD! Here I am, opening night. I actually made it through the day without fainting or vomiting or calling my mother for advice. The show has been going on for two acts now, and here I stand. All alone behind this piece of scenery. Waiting for my cue to come from the other side of this door. Standing patiently while I hear the rumblings of the other actors on stage. Yes, the other actors. Here I am, one of them. About to make theatrical history, ready to pounce onto that stage. Oh no. I think this time I really am going to be sick.

What's that? The audience, I can see the audience. I never realized this during rehearsals, but just beyond this piece of scenery and past the curtain, yes, it is the audience. And look who's there! Mr. Stanton, my 10th grade English teacher. "Put some feeling into it, man, this isn't a bedtime story; you're putting everyone to sleep!"

I never cared much for him after that. I'll show him who's putting who to sleep tonight. He'd remember me. I'll show him feeling. I've seen him here for other performances. Geez, I hadn't even thought about people being in the audience that I might know. There's Mary Ellen Bowman. Mary I-already-have-a-date-for-the-dance Bowman. I asked her out in the 11th grade, and she turned me down in front of the whole cafeteria. Giggling with all her girlfriends. Look at her now. Four kids, and the hips to prove it. I've avoided her all these years, and yet there she is. After tonight I know who she'll be wishing had taken her to the dance. And Joey Turnbay, my foreman at work. I didn't think his viewing went beyond Jerry Springer. Great, now everyone is going to hear about my performance tonight. But I don't care. I'm going to be great, that's right, just great.

Huh? Was that my cue? What did they say? Why is it so quiet? "I said, why don't we ask the butler?" Uuggh! That was my cue. C'mon you stupid door, open. Why won't it open, I'm turning the handle, why . . . pull, don't push. There it is, OK, now go out there. Walk out and face the audience.

I'm here, I'm on stage. Everyone is looking at me, the audience is looking at me, all eyes are on me! "Philipe, have you seen Mrs. Rhodes this evening?" I should answer here. This is the place. Now, say it now. "Why no, sir, I have not." I said it. I said my line. Look at them all hanging on my every word. I AM AN ACTOR AT LAST! The audience, the other cast members, the crew. At this very moment we have all connected.

"Philipe, I said you may leave now!"

Oh my God, that was the greatest single most exciting thing I have ever done. The rush of adrenaline. Without my one line, the show would have stopped. I kept it going. Kept the tension building.

I can't wait until the next audition. After a performance like this one, I'm sure to get three lines. Maybe four.

Five Years later . . .

Well, it's been five years since my first step onto the Capitol Civic Centre stage and I must confess, it has been a wild ride. Here I am in the wings for my seventh production. I can't believe I have been cast in every show I have auditioned for. Even after the broken chair incident, the small offstage fire, and the fall into the pit! I still get cast. God, I must be good. Well, I better get focused here; soon my cue will come for my first line. One of six I will deliver tonight. I am really on my way.

Solitaire

by
Bev Denor

The curtain opened with style (well, it didn't really open since there is no curtain in the cozy theater of the Forst Inn) on the Continental Greasepaint Company's annual production. The question is, what style was it?

Relying heavily on stock, cartoonlike characters, the actors maneuvered through the performance with little regard to the evident (albeit overworked) sentimentality of Mary Coyle Chase's award winning fantasy, Harvey. The show's most polished effort came from Manitowoc hometown diva Brenda Jacobson, although, in comparison to the rest of the ensemble, her errant displays of emotion resembled those of Oprah Winfrey (on acid).

Kudos to the design staff for offsetting the generally lackluster troupe with an impressive Victorian drawing room quite properly festooned.

Annie Walter's reviews of local theater productions always began just like that. Some wandering witticism (usually packaged parenthetically), followed by several biting remarks, and ending with a word seldom uttered in everyday conversation. Annie took her job as theater critic to *the Herald Times Reporter* seriously, too seriously, some thought. "I can make or break careers," she had been heard to say over lunch one day at the Colonial Inn. "A keystroke, that's all it takes, and an actor is either on her way or out the door."

Like Sardi's, the Colonial was the gathering place for local thespians. After rehearsals and performances, casts and crews would unwind with drinks and banana crème pie. Only the locals appreciated the Colonial. No one was bothered by the slanted floors or the primary yellow custard oozing over browning bananas. These never elicited comments, but Anne's remarks always did. Her "making or breaking" stars statement hit the rumor airwaves shortly after being uttered, and the reactions ranged from amusement to indignation. Yet, most who heard her pontificating realistically accepted that community theater was just that, community theater, and no one was going anywhere, with or without Annie's help.

Sitting before her laptop, Annie hesitated. She mused over the fact that her life had come full circle in a way. From teaching high school drama classes in Portland, taking on bit parts with regional professional companies, and then, after the divorce, returning to Manitowoc ("because of the climate," she always quipped) to raise her daughter and play the quintessential single parent. In reality, this was her hometown. She knew that in Manitowoc her daughter, Katharine, would be safe, get a good education, and hopefully develop a love of theater at Lincoln High School, just as Annie herself had done.

Upon her return, Annie discovered that the theater community had matured with the emergence of several new acting companies. Her bookstore job was a casual nine to five and so Annie had plenty of time to accept a position freelancing and writing theater reviews for the Herald Times Reporter (HTR). She often took Katharine with her on assignments, teaching her what was good and what was bad about each effort. Mostly bad.

Annie loved the rush of adrenaline that came with deadlines, and so she was in no hurry to get today's review done. After all, she had over two hours before she had to fax it off to the HTR.

Flipping the lid, she brought up her favorite program, Solitaire. For the longest time her obsessive-compulsive side needed one game a day, but over time that evolved into her play till you win strategy. Game one. A loss. Game two. Another loss. Three . . . finally!

"That's the deal," she told herself. "Now, settle in and write." Annie selected Microsoft Works and typed the slug *Our Town* in the upper left corner. Then she went to the kitchen to make coffee. She ground the beans, inhaling the addictive aroma as she sifted them tenderly into the filter. Adding cold tap water (hot diminishes the pungency) she mulled over her conversation with her editor.

"Why don't we send Nancy to review this one? She hasn't written a special in a while."

"No, really, I'm looking forward to this. Besides, I don't know if I could attend a play anymore without taking notes."

"I think you should just go and be a mom in the audience tonight. Enjoy the show and take some pressure off."

"You hired me for my professional background and my integrity, did you not?"

David knew he should simply pull her off of the review, but instead he continued to press. "When was the last time you felt any show was well done? Don't answer that . . . just rhetorical. If you suddenly crank out a glowing review, even if it is deserved, people will say it's because Katharine is playing the lead."

"Kate is just fine with this, and so am I, which is the real issue for you, isn't it?"

David hesitated. "Actually, yeah. I mean, you have a reputation for saying what you see, no softening the rough edges like your predecessor did."

"Let people say what they will. She's prepared and she's good. I've coached her myself, and yes, Mr. Editor, I can remain objective."

"May 11, 1999," she hammered beneath the slug. Annie took a long sip of her Jamaican Blue Mountain, reserved for events she called, "Creativity on Demand," and instinctively felt something missing. Music. Have to have music to write. After riffling through stacks of CD's, Annie loaded the player with some soothing Erykah Badu, a little reggae, and her favorite, Jimmy Buffett. Soon the review would be done, and she would be falling asleep considering Katharine in her first major role, Emily, in *Our Town*.

The selection of *Our Town* as the Masquers' winter show had not been without angst. Some thought it a show best left to high school groups while others fought hard to stray from the usual fare of saccharine musicals and urbane comedies by adding a classic to the lineup. The later group proved stronger and the naysayers generously reserved judgment until opening night.

The plush decor of the Capitol Civic Centre clashed with the stark set that greeted theatergoers. The director had taken a risk in playing the show against the brick stage wall, although doing so did support Wilder's desire to tear away all theatrical conventions, forcing viewers to examine their own lives, undressed and unashamed. The chandeliers are an oxymoron, she thought. Typical Thursday night crowd, lots of gray hairs, surely at least one will complain about not being able to hear.

She tried to visualize what was happening in the dressing rooms. The chills. The pacing. The annoyance. Inexperienced actors chatting and laughing. Incessantly. No respect for the seasoned cast's desire for quiet warm-up time and space. Been there. Been there. Been there. Done that. Hated it. She sighed and smiled.

Annie knew that the actor playing the Stage Manager would be frustrated with the main drape being open when the audience entered. He liked pacing his path before the show, running his lines in place, being alone and settling in until called into the green room. Not this time. With this show he would have to find some other way to navigate around the neophyte actors' energies. Including Katharine. Annie had named her after Katharine Hepburn.

Sitting in the audience that Thursday night, Annie fully expected to see signs of opening night jitters from the first-time actress. Instead, a perky, confident Emily Webb minced across the stage. No traces of her little Katie were to be found. Dialogue, flawless. Gestures, natural and meaningful. Facial expression and vocal interpretation, impressively understated. All this and more, Annie jotted into her notebook during the one hour and thirty-five minute opening act.

The audience was silent. They're listening to Thornton Wilder's words, his poetry, she thought. However, she found herself distracted by movement—crossing and uncrossing legs, shifting, the crackling of cellophane candy wrappers, and the sounds of people paging through programs.

At intermission Annie sat alone sipping merlot in the Kadow Hall. Her neighbors, Ron and Sharon, nodded at her and worked their way across the room. No one stopped or glanced her way, although she easily recognized twenty people in the hall.

"Hey, mother of the star."

"Nancy! I'm surprised to see you. Didn't you have plans for tonight?"

"Oh, sure, sure, but they fell through at the last minute so I figured I might as well use the HTR's review tickets and see . . ."

"Review tickets?" questioned Annie. "Dave understood that I would be reviewing this show, same as always."

Nancy awkwardly tried to conceal her notebook and pen behind her back. "Look, he asked me to be here in case things didn't . . . ah . . . well, he thought you might like to go to the opening night celebration afterwards rather than rushing home to pound out an article."

"Oh."

"So . . . what about it?"

"Thanks, Nancy. But I'll do it. I have a feel for this show, spent hours working with Katie on her lines, was in it in college, reviewed a professional production in L.A."

"Interesting play. I didn't know anything about it, but ya know, I'd sure like a little more scenery, and the pantomime, I just can't get into it. Did Masquers run out of money or something?"

"They had chosen to produce the show . . . "

"Hey, no offense, Annie. That's just me. Anyway, last chance."

"Thanks, but I'll do it."

"If you're sure. Then maybe I won't stay. I bet I can still catch Chris and Rick over at Kristina's and grab something for dinner. See ya."

"I thought you had plans . . . that changed . . ."

But Nancy was gone.

When the couple in front of her didn't come back after intermission, Annie was sure they had moved to better seats, a decision she was glad of since she now had a clearer view. As Annie noted brief descriptions of second act costume changes she became aware of a silence that was at first simply awkward, but gradually grew in intensity and volume.

Katie was lost. In the pivotal scene in Act Two, while George and Emily clumsily spoke their feelings to each other, Katie froze. Annie froze too, unable for a long time to glance up and see for herself what she knew was happening.

The actors sat near the lip of the stage, behind a soda fountain simply fashioned of a board bridged across the back of two wood chairs. Neither of the young performers knew what to say or where to look, but Annie was aware of Katie scanning the faces in first rows. She caught Annie's eye and averted her gaze, apologetically.

"Shit." Annie thought she had muttered that to herself, but maybe it had come from the wings.

The Stage Manager appeared and offered some inane remark about love in bloom; the two got their bearings and moved on. Annie felt a collective sigh of relief from the small audience. At the end of the act, when the minister pronounced them man and wife, Emily gave George a sweet, seventeen-year-old girl peck on the cheek, uncomfortable and unconvincing, hardly the first kiss of new bride. The audience chuckled.

She stepped out into the lobby for the second intermission. The crowd had thinned considerably since the first act and Annie had to admit that the show's pacing was off, and the production was running long, even for an amateur company. She found a private spot in the corner of the Kadow Hall and attempted to make more notes. Her mind wandered to the collection of photos on the wall. Theater royalty posing with such savvy that their star quality burned through the glass. And here she was, sadly watching her daughter sinking, unable to cast a lifeline, and acutely aware that there was one more painful act to come.

What would she say to Katie after the show? How would she approach her review? Annie slowly made her way back into the theater to watch the final act, her professional integrity beating incessantly in her aching heart.

Emily's burial and her introduction to the silence of the grave. Please let this flow, Annie prayed. But Act III went as anticipated. Embarrassing stutters. A cast under-rehearsed and too inexperienced to project the brilliance of Thornton's Wilder's theme. At the bow, the audience applauded politely and left.

Annie left quickly as well, feeling cold despite the unseasonably warm weather. The drive home was long, dizzying and lonely. Annie knew what she had to do. Surely Katharine would rush in, breathless with the excitement of her opening night "success."

"Well, what did you think, Mom? How was I? Come on, did you like it? What about the part where I . . .?"

Annie had already decided to let the review speak for her.

And so, without further hesitation, Annie Walters, the quintessential single mother and professional theater critic, settled her fingers comfortably on the home row of her Compaq Presario.

Let's see . . . black Queen on the red King . . . good start.

Five years later . . .

Annie Walters was assigned to cover an unconventional event taking place at the Manitowoc Expo, professional wrestling. She caught the eye of a mountain of a man called Lumberjack Louie and the two ran off shortly after and were married.

Katharine continued to perform in amateur theatrics. She went away to school, and, like her mother, she returned home. She teaches typing at Lincoln High School where she regularly and passionately lies to her students about her successful days on the stage.

In the Nick of Time

by
Emily M. Trask

As he hurried down the cold, gray walk, Jay's shoes beat a frantic cadence on the concrete. He inhaled and exhaled the dark January night air, watching his breath turning a thin, white powdered sugar before his red nose. He was late. Jay checked his watch again. "Why do I always have to be late?" he asked himself more as a reprimand than as a question. It was true, Jay was chronically late.

Auditions were being held for *West Side Story*. Jay loved the play. He'd read it about a hundred times, seen it on stage and in film almost as many, and practically wet his pants when the drama teacher announced they'd be doing it for the winter musical. With difficulty, Jay kept his cool, saying to his friends, "Well, I guess I'll try out since I've got nothing better to do. You guys should, too." His friends just laughed. But after a few days, they caved and scribbled their names below his on the sign-up sheet.

Jay couldn't fall asleep the night before auditions, and he felt the effects the next day. After school, his head kept bobbing just above his favorite late afternoon pick-me-up, a soggy bowl of Frosted Flakes. He decided to take a catnap since auditions first began at 6 p.m. But, when his lids snapped open, the clock read 6:42. He rubbed his eyes to make sure he wasn't still dreaming, and, realizing he wasn't, sprang to his feet and bolted out the door.

Breathless, he burst into the school auditorium. Forty-two heads spun around and focused dagger stares on his gasping form. He had interrupted Dex Sharridin's rendition of "Tonight, Tonight," and no one was pleased. He crawled to an empty seat and slunk down so low that the only evidence left of him was a stubborn tuft of mousy hair.

"I didn't know *Dex* was trying out!" Jay said to himself.

Dex and Jay had been best friends in grade school and junior high, but when they got to high school, Dex had changed. He couldn't afford to spend time with a "loser" like Jay. Those were

Dex's exact words. In addition to being a total prick, Dex had numerous other accomplishments: star receiver for the football team, tennis captain, president of the student senate, first chair trumpet (Jay was fifth), and a total ladies' man. And now Dex Sharridin was trying out for the lead in Jay's *West Side Story*. Unbelievable.

Dex finished and took a deep bow.

"That was excellent, Mr. Sharridin. I only wish I could apologize for the rudeness of other people," commented Mrs. Baker who then demanded, "Really, who was that who burst in?" Her eyes menacingly scanned the auditorium until they rested on the hair tuft in the back row.

"I'm sorry, I didn't know you were in the middle of an audition," Jay choked out.

"Well, these are auditions, so one might assume people would be . . . auditioning!" Mrs. Baker snapped.

Jay's face flushed.

"Well, are you here for the tryouts or aren't you?"

Jay stood, only to find his legs had turned to jelly. "I . . . I am," Jay stammered as he made his way to the stage.

Almost too quickly, the accompaniment began for "Maria." He took a deep breath and began boldly singing the first two lines. Yet, when it came time for the third line, Jay froze. He couldn't remember another word. So, at a loss, he sang the first two lines over and over and over. A wave of laughter rolled through the audience, and even Jay was chuckling himself in the end.

Although he'd made a late entrance to the auditions, and forgotten the words to his song, Jay was confident his voice quality had shown through and he would, at worst, get stuck in the chorus. Early the next morning, he and his friends crowded around the cast list. People took turns giving each other high fives and hugs when they saw their names printed under the "Jet" or "Shark" list. Jay waited for the chance to see his name. As he sauntered up, he saw "Dex Sharridin" boldly printed under the role of Tony. "I didn't really want that part anyway." He was still in high spirits as his eyes scrolled down the paper. He stopped at the last name, only to realize he had not read his own. Jay was not on the list.

His friends were cautiously sympathetic but soon drifted away. Jay stood alone for a moment telling himself there had to be some mistake. He had never wanted anything more than to be in this play. Later that day, in Act Lab, Dex breezed past Jay and muttered, "Looks like the little interruption backfired."

That was all Jay could take. He decided to march right into Mrs. Baker's classroom and demand that she straighten this mistake out. He made a beeline down the hall—a true man on a mission. But, as soon as he saw Mrs. Baker wearing her tightlipped scowl and brown polyester, Jay lost his nerve.

"May I help you, Mr. Crawford?" Mrs. Baker demanded as she pushed her glasses to the tip of her nose and peered over the rim.

"Yes, ummmm, I was wondering if by some chance . . . on the list . . . could you have forgotten . . . well, what I'm trying to say is . . ."

"Yes! What are you trying to say, Mr. Crawford?"

"Did you forget to put my name on the cast list?" He winced, waiting for the blow to strike.

"Let's see . . . Jay Crawford. No, I'm sorry, you weren't cast this time around." There it was: punch and follow through. Jay's heart sank.

"But I'll tell you what," Mrs. Baker continued in a less dismissive tone. "Mr. Nielson was looking for an extra hand or two in building the set. Maybe you could be of some help there."

Jay couldn't believe it! He hadn't made the play at all. It seemed so unfair. But, on the Monday following a full week of mourning, Jay heard an announcement for a set construction meeting after school. For some reason it sounded more enticing now than when the idea had come from Mrs. Baker's pursed lips.

At the meeting, Jay listened to Mr. Nielson, the school's art teacher, describe his vision for the set in excitingly minute detail. "Maybe this won't be so bad after all," Jay thought.

The next day, Jay went straight to the scene shop. Somehow, he still managed to arrive late and walked in just as Mr. Nielson was finishing up assigning jobs. " . . . and Jay Crawford, along with Mary Anne Kornelly, will be in charge of painting the backdrop."

The backdrop? It was huge and to be mostly olive green. Jay decided it was cruel and inhumane to make anyone look at that much olive green but got painting (with Mary Anne, who never took her headphones off). Boredom quickly set in, and his mind and the painting drifted from the task. Soon enough he was adding some decorative touches of his own. Before he realized it, Jay had painted a breathtaking scene. "Who did this?" demanded Mr. Neilson, silencing the room.

Jay sheepishly confessed.

Mr. Neilson stalked over to the backdrop, looked Jay straight in the eyes and asked, "Could you hear me when I said the backdrop was to be olive green?" Mary Anne lifted one headphone—things were about to get interesting. Then, without waiting for a reply, the teacher yanked the still wet paintbrush from Jay's hand, and in doing so splattered olive green all over the masterpiece. "Get out! Out!"

Jay walked slowly down the hall, past the vocal rehearsal rooms where, who else? Dex was working on one of his solos. He stopped in mid-note, just long enough to pop his head into the hall and sneer, "See ya around Picasso!"

Later that evening, the phone rang. To his surprise, it was Mr. Nielson.

"Jay, what I said this afternoon was unprofessional. I apologize."

"That's all right," Jay lied. "Does this mean I can come back on the set crew?"

"Well, how about this instead? Mr. Kozzel is desperate for help on the lighting crew."

Jay wrestled with the idea for a few days, but eventually made his way to Mr. Kozzel's classroom to volunteer for duty. Mr. Kozzel was, by far, the school's strangest teacher. He wore thick glasses, had a mop of tangled hair and an uneven mustache.

Jay casually inquired how many people would be working on the crew.

"Let's see now . . ." Mr. Kozzel paused for a moment. "There's me . . . and there's you and . . . that's it! Just me and you!"

It took Jay a while to learn the ropes, but Mr. Kozzel's vast knowledge of the technical aspects of theater and his gift for teaching made it easy. And actually fun. By the time they reached dress rehearsals, Jay was a pro.

Despite Jay's efforts to lose himself in his new life behind the scenes, the fact that Dex had the lead in his show still haunted him. Dex's constant taunting didn't help either. Not a day passed without Dex making some snide remark to Jay about the "awesome responsibility of turning on and off the lights."

Jay was determined to show Dex what an "awesome responsibility" it actually was. Jay had learned well from Mr. Kozzel and had designed a lighting plot that, with the push of a button and the help of a moving light, could make old Dex a sickly shade of puke green.

On opening night, Jay was late as usual. He burst in and made his way directly to the sound and light booth where Mr. Kozzel had everything under control. But Jay had opening night nerves and needed to use the restroom before the overture began. When he went to the men's bathroom, he was greeted by the sharp scent of urinal cakes and muffled sniffling. Dex was on the floor, whimpering like a baby.

Jay was pleased to see Dex in distress, but quickly changed his attitude when he saw the huge blue and purple bruise on the right side of his face. His lip was swollen and split in the middle. As he grimaced, Jay saw that one of Dex's teeth was chipped.

"I fell on the patch of ice outside of school and my face hit pretty hard. Does it look really bad, Jay?"

"Oh, once you put some makeup on it, no one will notice."

"I already did put makeup on! I'm going to look like an idiot. And tonight is the only night my dad will be in town to see the show."

For a moment, Jay just stood there. He knew that the bruises, coupled with his special lighting, and the yearbook photographer in the audience could even the score for years of insults he'd weathered. He savored the idea of Dex's public humiliation and the idea that he, Jay Crawford, held the power for revenge at his fingertips.

The show began. Everyone knew their lines; entrances and exits were smooth and perfectly timed. Jay had even cast a vibrant purple wash onto the olive green backdrop and brought it to life.

"Nice work!" Mr. Kozzel whispered. "A person can only take so much olive green." A few moments later, Dex made his first entrance. Jay immediately executed his cue and focused the spot directly on the show's leading man. But, instead of a sickly green as he had planned, Jay switched the color to a softer, forgiving peach at a lovely angle that cast shadows over the bruises. The light that flowed over Dex's face concealed his injuries. No one suspected that behind that smiling face, singing with convincing love for Maria, was a swollen, painful countenance.

Jay had decided not to tell anyone how he had "saved face" for Dex. But. When the yearbook came out, they both knew. And that was enough.

Five years later . . .

Dex Sharridin never did thank Jay for what he had done. After graduating high school, he entered the clergy and became a Jesuit priest and runs a mission in Brazil.

After a successful stint as a Broadway lighting designer, Jay Crawford decided to put his professional theater career to an early rest. He moved back to Manitowoc, Wisconsin and found his real calling as a teacher. His students claim Mr. Crawford is the greatest theater teacher who ever lived. For the upcoming year, Jay has chosen *West Side Story* as the spring musical.

The Switch

by
Gary Retzak

John Stepanski placed the phone back in its cradle on the kitchen wall. His wife, Linda, could tell from John's half of the conversation that Susan Janiak, the Masquers president, was informing him that his application to direct the fall musical, *The Sound of Music,* had been approved. This did not come as a surprise to her, nor should it have surprised John; he was the best director in the Masquers organization.

Seeing John's face change expressions from shock to surprise and then to a broad grin, Linda knew there was more important news. When John hung up, Linda set about coaxing the details from him.

"Was that Susan?" she asked.

"Yes, I'll be directing *The Sound of Music.*"

"You're not surprised, are you?" she asked.

"No, I'm not at least not . . . about that."

"Well, she must've said something unexpected, you're grinning like the Cheshire Cat."

"I don't know where to start! Susan also told me that the National Endowment for the Arts has a new program to promote community theater. The NEA looks for talented directors of community theater groups and gives them scholarships. Masquers submitted my name and I've been selected as a finalist."

"John, that's fantastic, you've wanted to go back to study theater for years! But what do you have to do to be chosen?"

"Well, I would be interviewed by some committee from the NEA. Next, the committee attends one of my plays and they make their decision based on the interview and the quality of the play."

John had a difficult time falling asleep that night. The more he thought about going back to school to study theater, the more excited he became. This opportunity would allow John to quit his job as a history teacher at Lincoln High School in Manitowoc,

Wisconsin, and pursue a job in a field he loved. Teaching was his livelihood. His passion, though, was theater.

John caught the bug when he played Nathan Detroit in *Guys and Dolls* in high school. He had wanted to major in Theater Arts at the University of Wisconsin, but his pragmatic father had talked him into a more practical career.

After earning his teaching license, he moved to Manitowoc to teach at Lincoln High School. One year later he auditioned for and was given a small part in a local production of *Gigi*. Since then, John participated in all aspects of community theater. In addition to acting, he constructed sets, managed props, worked as a stagehand, operated lighting, and applied makeup.

Five years ago, he began directing comedies and dramas. Three years ago, he tackled his first musical and by all accounts did an excellent job. John had been an active member of Manitowoc's oldest community theater group, the Masquers, Inc., for eight years. Masquers performs three shows a year at the Capitol Civic Centre, a grand old theater that boasts an orchestra section, a mezzanine, and a balcony. This Victorian Era theater seats approximately twelve hundred people.

However, the theater is also the source of the company's biggest headache. Masquers' audiences consistently complain that they are unable to hear all of the lines. In fact, Masquers members were divided on the cause of and the solution to the problem. Some believed that the theater had dead spots where sound was absorbed by surrounding structural materials. In fact, if someone were to use the scientific method to identify the seats in the dead spots, given sufficient time, the data would show that the entire house was a dead spot and that the average complainants were adults in their sixth decade.

A second group believed that the problem had nothing to do with dead spots but was caused by unschooled actors who didn't know how to project their voices. John sided with this group, with some reservations. Masquers rehearsals are held at the Coach House on the grounds of the Rahr West Museum. As a result, the thespians become accustomed to speaking at a volume suitable for the Coach

House, a space about the size of a three car garage. When the cast moves to the stage at the Civic Center a few nights before the production, the directors frequently need to remind the cast to turn up the volume. On opening night, the actors voices' are competing with background noises composed of coughs, sneezes, air conditioners, squeaky chairs, spotlight cooling fans, and the whispers of gray haired men asking their wives to repeat the last line.

"What are you going to do about the sound system?" Linda asked.

"I'm going to convince Masquers to rent body mics."

Linda recalled John's last campaign to bring technology to Masquers. In 1989, he convinced the organization to buy floor microphones. These were set downstage close to the orchestra pit. The results were disappointing. The microphones helped when the performers were downstage, near the microphones, and facing the audience. But when they were looking to the wings or upstage, the microphones were not sensitive enough to pick up the voices. In fact, the microphones caused some performers to get lazy. They believed there was no longer any need to project.

With a look of concern on her face Linda replied, "In *Anything Goes* the microphones did such an excellent job of amplifying the orchestra that you couldn't hear the singers' voices. And during the tap dances, the floor mics made the four tap dancing sailors sound like the entire Riverdance troupe."

"At least no one complained about not being able to hear the orchestra or the tap dancers!"

Over the next few days John obsessed over the sound problem. After considering a number of options, he decided to rent body mics for the show. Wireless microphones had become readily available, and John viewed this technological advance as a godsend—the final solution. After all, he thought, all the traveling companies were using them so they must be the answer. Four days before opening night, the cast had their first opportunity to rehearse on stage. John and the cast waited for the body mics with great anticipation: John, because he was anxious to solve the sound problem and to further his own career; the lead actors and actresses, because they believed that using body mics gave them a certain status. It put them in the big leagues. Rehearsals were held on Sunday and Monday nights.

During Act One of the final rehearsal, a few of the women in the cast had problems with widely varying volume levels. During intermission, John did some investigating to determine the cause. He noticed that the women who were having this problem all had their microphones attached to their shoulder. John deduced that when their heads were turned toward the mic, their voices were amplified too well. When their lines were spoken with their heads turned toward the other shoulder, the microphones could barely pick up their voices.

"Why is your microphone attached to your sleeve?" he asked the Duchess.

She answered by unclipping the mic from her left shoulder and reattaching it to the centerline of her Bavarian costume. "Look," she said, "if I attach it here, it hides my cleavage. Why should Masquers pay lots of money to rent this great costume only to hide my boobs!"

John turned to the person in charge of costumes and said, "Joan, see if you can hide the microphones in their cleavages. Maybe you could clip it to their brassieres or something."

"Why don't you show us how?" the Duchess exclaimed while offering her ample bosom up to John. "I don't want any lumps to show!" she called out to him as he walked away.

During Act Two the problem seemed to disappear. John was pleased with the results and announced to the producers that he had the problem licked.

Wednesday night was a dark night for the cast. On opening night, through the first few scenes of Act One, the lead players could be heard well no matter where they stood on stage. John, pacing at the back of the theater, was nearly beside himself with delight at having finally solved the problem. He visualized the wonderful accolades printed in the *Herald Times Reporter* . . . "This delightful show, directed by the talented John Stepanski, is a must see . . . and

John is the first director of a local production who has been able to direct a play wherein every member of the cast can be heard."

Toward the middle of Act Two, as John mentally composed his letter of acceptance to the NEA, it became obvious that the solution had created another problem. An evening that started so well turned out to be the worst of his directing career.

It began when Baroness Elsa Schraeder exited the stage at the close of scene one and headed for the dressing room. On the way, she bumped into Kurt Von Trapp, who was just coming from the green room.

"Hi Kurt! How do you think the show is going so far?"

Kurt replied in a confidential tone, "I think the show's going all right, but these lederhosen are too tight in the crotch and they're killing me! How do German men wear these things?"

"Kurt, I think you've discovered the real cause of World War II . . . a bunch of grumpy German men wearing lederhosen."

"I don't know about that, but I do know where the phrase up tight came from."

"Sounds to me like those lederhosen are made like a cheap hotel . . . no ballroom."

Kurt and the baroness had a couple laughs over his predicament and they moved on. Unfortunately, after the baroness left the stage she had forgotten to turn the microphone transmitter off. The audience roared as the baroness's conversation regarding Kurt's costume mixed with the actors' stage lines.

It wasn't until the cheap hotel joke that John woke up from his reverie. By that point the conversation between Kurt and the baroness was over and John wasn't sure if his ears had tricked him. He looked to the audience for reassurance. They all seemed to be enjoying the show—so he did nothing. Had he been paying closer attention, he would have realized the audience was laughing hysterically, although inappropriately, while Maria explained her situation to the Mother Abbess.

After the laughter died down and John was imagining himself as a famous Hollywood director, the baroness entered the small ladies' room next to the dressing rooms below the stage.

Audience members thought they heard thunder. It was November, snow was on the ground, so thunder was highly unlikely. But there was thunder quickly followed by the sound of a solid water stream.

John's face turned a deep shade of purple, his eyes bulged. The veins stood out at the base of his neck. John then dashed backstage to find the offending party. He ran through the dressing rooms looking for someone whose microphone might still be on. Within minutes he checked all the leads. He knew Maria was on stage, so he narrowed down to Elsa.

"Where's Elsa?" he yelled as he ran through the dressing rooms again.

"In the john . . . ahhh, the ladies' room" Brigitta replied.

John ran to the ladies' room and began knocking quietly on the door. Afraid that his voice would carry, he whispered as loudly as he could "Turn off your mic!"

"What?"

"I said, turn off your damn mic."

"Who the hell is that? What're you doing hanging around outside the ladies' room?"

Elsa flushed the toilet. As she washed her hands she said, "John, is that you? What were trying to tell me through the door that couldn't wait? I'm not late for an entrance am I?"

As Elsa opened the door, John pounced upon her and heatedly rummaged beneath her gown feeling for the transmitter.

". . . hey, get your hands off my butt, you're a happily married man!

Unable to find the transmitter, John quickly dropped her skirt, stood up and plunged his hand down her cleavage. He pulled out the microphone covering it with his hand. He whispered to Elsa, "Your . . . damn . . . microphone . . . is . . . still . . . on! Turn it off now!"

Elsa registered shock at John's uninvited invasion of her bosom, but then she realized that everything she had said, and even worse, done, since leaving the stage had been broadcast to the audience. She quickly reached under her skirt and flipped the switch to OFF.

Mother Abbess arrived. "Who the hell was having a pee while I was singing?" Recognizing guilt on Elsa's face she screamed, "You ruined my scene! It was supposed to be serious and the entire audience was laughing at you farting and peeing! You will never be in another play with me again!"

It was over. The scholarship had gone up in flames. Down the dumper really, John thought to himself. There was nothing left to do. He found an empty dressing room, slid into a chair.

As John hung his head in his hands and sobbed shamelessly, the audience gave Kurt and Elsa the only standing ovation they would receive during the show's entire run.

Five years later ...

John has taken up golf.

Ships That Pass

by
Brad Zimmermann

The blare from the maroon Taurus's horn snapped me back to the task at hand. I was running late again and tonight that just wouldn't do. Tonight was the night—-opening night. Time to take the baby so many had worked on, nourished, and perfected, and introduce it to the world.

The brakes of my gray Horizon groaned as I stopped at the intersection. I looked at the clock in my dashboard. Damn! 5:25. I still had an hour's worth of interstate ahead of me and thirty-five minutes to do it in. Well, I loved a challenge. I guess maybe that's why I love Deanne, I mean loved. I keep forgetting that.

Speeding down the I-43, the hum of my tires began to ease my tension and lull me into a state of relaxation, much like a double vodka tonic.

Thoughts of Deanne flooded my consciousness. Deanne had always fallen asleep to the sound the tires make as they roll endlessly against the asphalt. She had loved that sound, loved a lot of things, but in the end not me, not like I wanted her to. It's funny how some memories fade quickly into the background like the static of an empty radio frequency. Yet others take root and hold on, staying clear, crisp, and strong, fed by some unknown, unconscious force.

God, where had it all started, how did it go wrong, and where had it ended? I've been asking myself for over a year. Is there ever a real answer when a two-sided emotion turns into a one-sided battle?

I had met Deanne over three years ago. We were playing opposite each other in Shakespeare's *A Midsummer Night's Dream*. I had played Oberon to her Titania. We had hit it off almost immediately becoming fast friends, best friends, yet not comfortable friends. Oh, we would go out together, get a bite to eat, or just sit and bitch about life. But there always seemed to be a tension between us. The kind of tension, I realize now, two people share when they both know eventually friends will become lovers. I think we both had felt that from the beginning, but the situation had been sticky then—Deanne in a bad marriage she desperately wanted out of, and myself brought up too Catholic to push the issue.

I remember the night that I fell in love with Deanne. It had been opening night of the show and she had just come off of stage left and headed back to the changing rooms. God, she was breathtaking that night. Her long black hair brought up at the sides, the rest of it falling down over her back like a lazy ebony river. Against the dark canvas of her hair her blue eyes looked all the more radiant, taking on the shade seen only in an Alaskan lake, an endless blue whose depths one can only wonder about. Deanne's gown, a masterpiece of airy white lace and Austrian crystal beads, hung off her petite frame with all the grace and delicacy of a spider's web misted with dew. The rhinestone crown atop her head glittered arrogantly, giving her just the right amount of regal elegance, making her look quite literally like the Queen of the Fairies. Yes, she was beautiful, enchanting. In her eyes was a distant look of loneliness and pain. It was a look I could all too easily recognize and identify with. As she passed me that night we locked eyes. At that moment a connection was made, one I would come to both relish and regret.

After the play Deanne and I went for coffee at the Premiere Café up the road from the theater. We both ordered a latte and grabbed a small table outside toward the back of the stone terrace. The stars peeked through the holes of our living roof, a canopy of morning glories and orange trumpet vine held aloft by delicate yet sturdy wrought iron trellises. It was late August and the night was clear and cool. A slight wind was blowing in from the lake bringing the heavy scent of water and the distant call of the lighthouse. Our conversation drifted from one surface topic to the next, finally to settle on the show, its production, and the people in it. God, we had so much in common. We liked the same parts in the show, laughed at the same jokes, and we both found Larry Somners, the stage manager, to be an anal-retentive bore.

The evening passed quickly and soon Dan, the café owner, was cleaning up and telling us it was time to close. Deanne and I stood on the sidewalk in front of the café. I remember how awkward it all felt. Not quite sure how to say goodbye. We both stood like teenagers on our first date, wanting desperately for the other to give some clue or to have the courage to make the first move. Neither of us did.

We kept in touch, in fact in the months that followed we saw quite a bit of each other. In the beginning it had taken awhile to get her to open up but once she did we talked and shared a lot. Deanne explained to me about the complicated relationship she shared with her husband, about their courtship and eventual marriage. She talked about the love that she once had for him and how that love seemed to vanish so quickly after the I-dos. I listened patiently, shamelessly offering my support and shoulder. Of course, I told myself that I was doing this all selflessly, but I knew better. With every piece of advice I offered, I felt a pang of guilt, knowing my motives weren't truly noble. Now honestly, I did want to be a good friend to her, she needed one, but I couldn't deny the love that was growing stronger in me every day.

I took for granted our easy relationship until, inexplicably, Deanne stopped calling. After two weeks of silence, I picked up the phone and dialed her number. No answer. I was worried. I started asking around and eventually found out that Deanne had left her husband and gotten an apartment in town. I was hurt. I couldn't believe she didn't let me know about such a big decision, that she wouldn't let me help. But I guess that was Deanne, at least a part of her. She never wanted to ask for help, always so stubborn in thinking she could shoulder things alone. I was surprised, though, that she hadn't called. Did I mean that little to her? Had all the late night conversations we shared meant nothing? Why hadn't she called?

The ringing in the hall awakened me from a sound sleep. I rushed from the warmth of my bed into the chill air to answer my phone, knocking the picture of my sister from the wall in the process. I remember being afraid to answer. I mean, let's face it, in most cases a phone call late at night usually spells trouble. My hand shook slightly as I put the receiver to my ear.

"Hello," I had said uncertainly.

"Can I come over?" Deanne's voice trembled out.

"Deanne, what's wrong?"

"I just can't be alone tonight, can I spend the night?" I could hear the tears in her voice.

I pulled back the curtain hanging over my front window feeling the heavy green brocade cloth in my hands. I stood looking out into the inky black night. It had been warm that day, pleasantly so, a nice surprise for the end of November. Deanne's Buick Skylark pulled into my driveway twenty minutes later. I watched her climb from the car. She seemed to be moving in slow motion. Deanne never said a word as she stepped through my door. She just looked at me with hollow, defeated eyes, dropped her black overnight bag to the floor and fell into my arms crying. A while later her tears stopped and the embrace, which began as one of comfort, quickly changed to one of desire. Our lips found each other and the feelings the two of us had always managed to keep caged broke free and were roaming wild. The love we made that night was urgent and unrestrained. Emotion danced between us like the lightning of a summer storm. And the torrent seemed to last for hours. Afterwards we lay in each other's arms, each heavy breath conveying emotion a million words could never explain.

I never did ask her what was wrong. Jesus, that seems odd to me now. I do know however that it would not have mattered what her explanation was. I would be there for her as I always had been, unquestioning, unconditionally there. Looking back, I should have seen the danger in behavior like that.

We parted almost silently the next morning, neither of us knowing what to say about the previous night.

I felt like I was living a dream. I felt so happy, so free and alive. Never had I experienced an emotion like this. I wanted to lose myself in this dream. Yet, somewhere in the darker corners of my mind a voice was saying, "Eventually, dreams end." I would not think of that now. For the first time in my life, I was happy.

Happy, that's what I told myself for weeks after that night. Deanne and I were still sleeping together but the dynamics of our relationship had changed. She seemed to be slowly pulling away from me, becoming distant and moody. Gone were the days when conversation flowed easily. I had never needed to think of what to say to Deanne but now I did, and our talks seemed forced and stiff.

Deanne's phone calls became more and more infrequent. Had I done something wrong? Was I somehow not good enough? I tried to talk to Deanne about us but every time I did she became evasive and quiet. I couldn't figure out how to get through to her. What was wrong? Was she afraid? Were the emotions too strong or not strong enough? I drove myself crazy day and night. But in the end I decided to stop thinking about it. I figured as long as Deanne kept coming to my bed things would work out, it would be okay; Deanne loved me.

It's amazing what love can convince you of, make you blind to. I fought like a soldier on the front lines obsessed with victory. Even though the odds were against me and I knew the battle couldn't be won, I still kept on fighting, dumb enough to believe love would conquer all. What a fool I was to think love was all that mattered. The only place that's true is in the movies.

Our relationship ended in direct contrast to how it started, at least on her part. It had been weeks since I had talked to or seen Deanne. I left messages on her machine that she never saw fit to return. I wrote her letters explaining how I felt. They went unanswered as well. I should have gotten the picture but, as dumb as it sounds, I still had hope that maybe she loved and cared about me and just needed time to figure things out.

My answer came three weeks and two days later. Deanne called me up and said four deadly words. "We need to talk."

I waited at my apartment pacing. I made half-hearted attempts to tell myself that this would be okay, this wouldn't be the end, but deep down I knew better. When the knock came I walked slowly, deliberately. I swear somewhere far off I heard a voice call, "Dead Man Walking." I don't remember much about our talk other than the phrase, "I don't love you. I never did."

I took the news like a man, never flinching, never showing emotion and never shedding a tear, at least not in front of her. After

Deanne left I closed and locked the door, sank to the floor and let the tears come. I had never felt anything like the pain and ache I had in the center of my chest where my heart had been. I found it difficult to breathe. I prayed that the tears would somehow dilute the pain. I just sat on my couch and tried to make some kind of sense out of all of it. It's like standing in the middle of ground zero and trying to figure out where to start and how to rebuild. We went our separate ways. I thought about her all the time and grieved for what I had lost. I went into a self-imposed exile to lick my wounds and start the healing process.

Eventually, I started to live again. I got in touch with old friends and started going out and even got involved in our community theater again. It had been over a year since I had last seen or talked to Deanne. I had my life and she had hers. The overwhelming pain I had felt had ebbed a bit. I learned to live with it, and in some ways, respected it; it was a reminder to be careful.

And that brings me to tonight—opening night of our production of *Man of La Mancha*. I snagged the lead. It's been a challenge and a lot of work, but it's been rewarding. The clock in my dash says 6:15. Only fifteen minutes late, not bad.

The backstage is in complete chaos as I step from my dressing room. People running here and there, the props guy screaming because he can't find that "darn red scarf." Everyone seems nervous and on edge; usually I would be, too, but tonight I feel completely calm and in control.

Someone yells "places" and the orchestra begins the overture. I take my place on stage left and wait for the lights to blaze to life and the curtain to rise. The orchestra is on its last song when I look to see my leading lady take her place across the stage.

Deanne smiles looking arrogant dressed in the whore costume of Dulcinea. I give her a good luck wink just as the curtain goes up.

Yes, quite often when we least expect it fate steps in and throws people back into the mix together. Whether it's for the good or for the bad remains to be seen. But in the end life is a great play, we her characters, fate our script, and destiny . . . the stage.

Five years later . . .

I remained saddened, haunted really, by the thought of what could have been for Deanne and me. In fact, I became so troubled and unable to face the daily possibility of bumping into her, that, at age thirty-five, I ran away. To ensure that no one would ever find me, I changed my name to Dion. And I am proud to say that I am the only Peninsula Player ever to be billed by a single name.

Deanne continued to act in Manitowoc productions, staying close to home to raise her five children. When she did venture out, it wasn't far. On one such outing, she found herself in a quaint coffee shop in Egg Harbor where she spotted me across the room sampling the chocolate dipped espresso beans. By the time she made her way over, I was gone, but my companion remained. "Excuse me, I know this is rude," she began, "but could you tell me your friend's name, please?"

"Dion," he replied, and strolled away.

Touchdown

a love story

by
Bev Denor

"**S**onofabitchsonofabitchsonofabitch." Moby was on his feet screaming at the TV. All alone. His rickety arthritic legs bent at the knees and he hopped ever so slightly into the air with each sonofabitch.

Moby's anger swelled. His feeble arms tore at his green and gold sweatshirt. Tugging and tugging, the shirt eventually twisted above his head, sending Moby into a frenzied circle dance of frustration as he labored. Finally successful, he threw it to the ground, red faced. Short of breath. And then Moby did something he hadn't done for eight years. Since he returned home from Sylvia's burial refusing to face his grief. He cried. An animal sound rose from deep in his gut pushing through to his throat and bursting.

Moby sank onto the couch and beat his fists on the worn cushions bringing up billows of dust. Coughing now, and still crying he agonized, "You call yourselfs a football team. Bullshit. You play like pansies. I'm done with yous. Waste a my time." Then, out of the crying, the coughing, and the swearing came a little laugh. Gentle at first, then growing to a cacophonous symphony of rapture and reckless abandon. Moby was whole again. Healed by Superbowl XXXII.

In that short passage of time, Moby was reunited with his emotions. Emotions that had been dormant. There had been no anger. No laughter. No tears. No hope, no caring. no giving, no loving and no reason. But in this overwhelming snap, he felt them all again. And something else. The emotions shot-gunnned through him. Rat-a-tat-rat-a-tat-rat-a-tat. Reminding him of himself and of life. And then he bolted upright and became quiet.

"What the hell . . ." A tingle. A twitch. Can't be, he thought. "Jesus." And with that Moby decided it was time to clean himself up and get laid.

By Tuesday next, Moby was looking and smelling pretty good. He had managed to loofah off most of the dried skin that had been left unattended and itchy for far too long. He washed and ironed a shirt, dug out a belt, and was looking quite spiffy even though he insisted on tightening the belt below his jiggly belly rather than locating his waist and fastening it there. But he was clean, comfortable.

In section B, page 2 of the *Herald Times Reporter,* Moby discovered the smiling face of Christine, inviting him to audition for Heart-A-Rama, a sort of variety show fund raiser for the Wisconsin Heart Association. She was tiny and blond. Immediately Moby thought about Martha Stewart. He had always been a little hot for her. Watching her roll marzipan balls between her lightly greased palms, rolling and caressing, caressing and tenderly telling viewers how marzipan is delicate and must be respected if one is to get full flavor from it made him quiver. He thought about how she prepares her garden each spring. Sifting soil delicately between her fingers, scooping it up again and again doing what she knew the soil needed before she could properly plant.

Well, if Christine wants me, he thought, she shall have me. Besides, he had spent most of Sunday night and all of Monday making a list of where to find women. He called his daughter, good-for-nothing Julia. Of course he couldn't come right out and tell her what was on his mind, so naturally the middle-aged wart got the wrong idea.

"Dad," she began. "We could get you in to talk with someone. You seem . . . stressed."

Of course he was stressed. He hadn't had sex in eight years, maybe more. Sylvia was pretty busy her last few years. Didn't want to be bothered. He was ready to explode with stress.

"Damn it, I don't need to talk to anyone. I just need to know where people go. And don't tell me the Senior Center. That's just a bunch of deaf old women painting flowers on empty eggshells. Don't need that shit."

He had one goal in mind, but he couldn't figure out where or how to attack. Until perky little Christine. The answer to his needs.

Oh, sure the article said that she was producer of the show, and her husband was one of the directors. She was married. But Moby didn't want a long-term thing. She was cute. And besides, he had heard about those theater people and how, in the heyday of vaudeville, they weren't allowed to spend the night in most towns. They slept in train cars traveling from booking to booking. There was a reason for that. They were all promiscuous. And his little Christine might be, too.

The audition was painless. A little reading. Some dance steps (that was the only hard part), and then he sang "Happy Birthday." Christine ran the audition and within 45 minutes she told everyone to go home. "Don't call us, we'll call you." Moby got the message. Maybe he had splashed on a bit too much Jade East. Everyone around him seemed to be coughing. And, he had farted while he waited for his turn. But he couldn't help it.

On Thursday, Moby got a call from someone named Jenny. She wanted him to be in a tweener (whatever that was). He would be part of a chorus of singing cranberry bushes. He accepted even though he was puzzled by the concept of a chorus of cranberry bushes. He didn't want to ask questions and look too stupid. Besides, now he'd be seeing a lot of Christine.

Moby was nervous at the first meeting, but he bonded quickly with a guy named Chip, a sort of sexually ambiguous diva-type. Chip teased Moby, which drew attention to him. Moby learned early that when Chip teases, well, in the world of lakeshore community theater, that's as powerful as the Good Housekeeping Seal of Approval.

A May-December thing soon developed between them. Chip told Moby who was who and what was what. Stay away from this one . . . don't believe a word that one says . . . he's a baker . . . she's a lawyer . . . stuff like that! Moby figured that Chip could help his dear old pal cozy up to Christine. In the process he also thought he could straighten Chip out, so to speak.

After the first rehearsal, Moby glided into his driveway humming what he could remember of the song they had been learning. No matter how hard he tried he just couldn't get the transition into the chorus right. He wanted to be perfect so that he would be asked back next year. That's the way it works, Chip had told him. Learn your stuff, don't piss anybody off and you're in as long as you want to be. OK. Moby glanced at his watch. He'd been home for fifteen minutes. Chip was home by now too. He'd call him about the song.

The phone rang and continued to ring until "Hi, this is Chip, leave a message."

God, how Moby hated those things. He never knew who was at the other end listening or how much to say or how loudly. He always opted for real loud.

"Hello?" he shouted tentatively. "This is Moby. Tell Chip I called. About the song. I can't remember if the second part goes like this . . ." Here he broke into an off key rendition of "Wasting away again in this cranberry bog . . ." (a Buffett song with lyrics adapted to fit the occasion, but Moby hadn't figured that out yet). "Is that how it goes?" he hollered. "Call me back and let me know. My number is on that sheet that lady gave us tonight."

Moby didn't really understand how the whole thing was going to work. He knew that he was a small part of something real big and he wanted to do his best. The next morning, he went out to buy a book. Now this was something he hadn't done in a long time, if ever, so Moby wasn't quite sure where to go. He stopped at City News. Last time he had been there it was called the Karmel Korn and, in addition to the store's namesake, they sold books and magazines. The new owner added videos, but he didn't have what Moby wanted. He suggested a nearby store. Moby discovered that the store owner knew a bit about theater and so he described his new venture. Starring role. Wanted to shine. Needed to learn it all quickly. In no time he was headed home with a copy of Uta Hagen's *Respect for Acting.*

As he reached into his pocket for change, Moby found the cast list with everyone's names and addresses. Chip hadn't called him back. Maybe the machine forgot to give him the message. As long as he was out and about, he'd just stop by; maybe practice their song together.

When Moby arrived, Chip was making an omelet. He was wearing pumps!

"Hey, Moby," he chirped. "I was planning to call when I finished brunch. Eat yet?

He hadn't and so Chip invited him to share the omelet. A copy of *Bon Appétit* lay on the counter and Chip referred to it as he worked.

"You know, Moby, this is sort of a special occasion. Your first play and all. What do you say we get crazy and have a little mimosa with our breakfast?"

Again Moby found himself in the dark. No clue what mimosa was. "Sounds great."

"It's nice to have company," Chip said. "I'm usually here alone." As he talked, he flitted around the room, opening cupboards and drawers, pulling things together until he and Moby were seated at a tastefully set glass top table. He had divided and flipped the perfect omelet onto two handblown, cobalt blue breakfast plates. These he set atop natural fiber placemats and handed Moby a matching napkin in a ring of handmade paper. Chip caught the puzzled expression.

"Oh, it's nothing really. Carol Duvall, you know, on HGTV, made paper one day and it looked like fun, so I tried something simple. You like?"

Moby wasn't sure how to react to Chip in his pumps talking like, well, acting like, actually, Martha!

"Sure, they're real nice, Chippy. Real nice." He kept worrying that Chip would fall over in his shoes, but he seemed skilled.

By the time Moby figured out what mimosa was, it was too late. Chip told Moby stories about people in Heart-A-Rama, stories he shouldn't have told. And Moby laughed until his bladder couldn't take it and he dribbled. That made him laugh harder.

"Moby, look at the time. 12:30. Hey, let's go to a movie."

"OK, what's on? Arnold Schwarzenegger is my favorite. Is he playing?"

"Don't think so. How about *Bridget Jones's Diary?*"

Before they left, Chip opened a Cadbury Milk Tray to share with Moby. Bridget's favorite treat (But only people who read the book know this!) And they were off!

On Monday they rehearsed. Tuesday Moby called Chip, and they went out for coffee. Moby had his first cappuccino, and the experience made him feel French (sure Chip told him cappuccino is Italian in origin, but he still felt French!) and philosophic.

"We'll get to them, won't we? Me and you. We're pretty good together."

"You never know, Moby. This is the way it goes. Some nights the audience is with you, other nights you'll think the audience forgot to show up. That's just the way it is."

"But they'll like us won't they? I mean, I know they'll judge, but they'll like us."

"Don't count on it. There will be a couple of cranks who will have to find fault. Don't kid yourself."

"Well, you know what Uta says about that."

"Whooota?"

"Uta. Uta Hagen. You know, the actress from *Who's Afraid of Virgina Woolf?*"

"That was Elizabeth Taylor."

"And Uta Hagen"

"OK. And Uta Hagen." So what does Uta Whoota say?"

"She said, oh hell, now I can't remember but I marked it while I was studying."

Chip just let that comment pass.

"I'm studying theater."

"Moby, you kill me. This is Heart-A-Rama. You don't need to know the "method" or to have motivation. You just need to know your lines. This is not, I repeat, not theater."

"Wait, wait, " he thumbed through his already tattered copy of *Respect for Acting*. "Look, she says 'More than in any other performing arts the lack of respect for acting seems to spring from the fact that every layman considers himself a valid critic.' Why is that, do you think?"

"Hell Moby, I don't know. Maybe because they don't understand what we do. I personally find myself fascinating and all my performances riveting. That's all that matters. Drink your cappuccino and don't worry about it."

Moby brought the cup to his lips, trying to slurp through the feathery topping but it tickled. He laughed, the froth shot up his nose and all over his face.

"Jesus Christ," he muttered slapping his forehead in the characteristic gesture Chip had learned to expect each time Moby got himself tangled or frustrated.

On Wednesday Moby went to the library and read an article about Minnie Driver in *People Magazine*. In it she said that it's too big of a responsibility to look pretty in films, especially when people know that in real life you resemble a "sack of potatoes." Moby liked that. He knew he wasn't handsome or charming. But he still would be the best cranberry bush on that stage. Chip failed to see the point when Moby called him with the revelation, but he was glad to hear from him just the same.

Three weeks passed. The flurry of activity dizzied him. New people to know. Moby learned words to songs and found out that on stage, left is right and up is back, or something like that. Mostly he just wandered and hoped that eventually he'd get to the right spot. And he was sure to flash his Uta Hagen every chance he got.

Finally, Moby had his first real encounter with Christine. She was in charge of the dress rehearsals, bringing each individually rehearsed skit together into a smooth flowing unit. She hadn't been at any of the cranberry practices, but she would be at all of the performances. All nine of them. Three weeks had been a long time. But he had been loyal to his fantasy. However, he was burning. Watching Martha polishing her silverware hadn't helped his situation either!

"See you tomorrow, Chippy," Moby said as they left the final dress rehearsal.

"So, are you ready for this, Mobs? Won't be too much for the old ticker will it?"

"Oh ya, the ticker's just fine. There's other parts a me need some tuning up. Get it?" He elbowed Chip in the ribs.

"Jeez Moby, how I could not get it. What was up with you tonight? Everybody was watching, and I must say, I was a little embarrassed."

"Embarrassed?"

"The way you were sniffing around Chris all night. You lit her cigarette. You picked up her pencil. You stared at her butt when she bent to tie her shoe. You were so obvious."

"Oh. Well. I was hoping . . . "

"I know what you were hoping. But you gotta drop it. There is no hope there. Get it?"

"But I burn, Chip."

"So do I, Moby."

"Really?"

And they went their separate ways.

On the morning of opening night, Moby was up early, showered and shaved. At 9 a.m. he switched on Martha Stewart and watched her make a turban by sewing two of her midsized Martha by Mail towels together. How he loved that woman. A little bit fleshy around the midsection from childbirth and fine dining. She smiled coyly and tilted into the camera. Her lips were wet with excitement as she announced, "Now I will show you how to correctly put on your turban." And she bent over. The top two buttons of her shirt were undone. Moby was sneaking closer to the set to see if he could get a peek at her cleavage when the phone rang.

"Ya," he bellowed, thinking it was his good-for-nothing daughter Julia, calling to counsel him about some thing or the other.

"Hey, buddy, ya ready for tonight?"

"Oh hey, Chipper, sure, sure. How's about you?"

"Been there.

"Done that," Moby finished for him. Boy, we really are a team, he mused.

"Listen, I'll pick you up. Parking gets a little crazy so the less cars the better. Around 6:15."

He hung up before Moby could thank him. Chip had been awfully nice to him, Moby thought. Tonight he would stick close to Chip, let him know how much all his help was appreciated. Maybe he'd buy him a shot of flaming Yukon and they could laugh and tell dirty jokes like guys do sometimes. Yeah, yeah, that's a good plan. Make Christine wonder if I'm mad at her. She'll be around in no time, he figured.

Chip arrived as scheduled, and the boys cruised out to put on the show. Moby sang, "You Gotta Have Heart," the show's theme song, at the top of his lungs.

"You're obnoxious."

"Huh?"

"I'm just warning you. You're being a pain in the ass. And if you keep it up I'm done taking care of you."

Chip had grown attached to Moby. Liked him a lot, really, and wouldn't have abandoned him for the world. And he was happy that Moby was popular in the group. People enjoyed the funny old guy who didn't know his way around the stage and didn't know enough about theater royalty to know who to gush over yet, so to be on the safe side he just schmoozed with everyone. People liked watching him step on toes, move right instead of left, and all particularly enjoyed Moby enjoying the coed dressing room.

"Never saw so much underwear," he said to Chip. "When did Christine change? I missed it."

Moby made a mental note to buy new underwear.

The evening flew and soon Moby and Chip were in place for their skit. Chip remembered his first time. The twisted stomach, shortness of breath, the false start on his first song . . . those feelings came dancing back to him, except this time the nervousness and the excitement were for Moby. Chip wanted this to be great for him. He looked at the stubby old guy, bouncing a little, then swaying and then muttering as he got ready for his big moment. And then, right before they made their entrance, Chip put a hand on Moby's shoulder and whispered, "Break a leg."

After that Moby was on his own. He was in his cranberry suit, singing and dancing. Moving left when everyone else moved right. Having a great time just being alive. In the background, Chip watched with satisfaction. He had gotten Moby to this point. He had diverted Moby's attention from Christine, he was sure, and introduced him to the sheer pleasure of playing. He felt perfect joy watching his friend.

The skit ended, and shortly, the entire cast was on stage singing the closing number. Oh, there was a standing ovation and the customary kissing, hugging among the cast. Moby was speechless, filled with pride, although somewhat exhausted. He had made people laugh. He had accomplished something grand. Something he had never dreamed of doing before. Before he wanted to get laid and before he fell for Martha and then Christine. But Chip was the one who truly moved him. Moby decided to change clothes quickly and find a private place to give Chip a small thank you gift, a hand tooled leather purse from St. Vinnie's.

The anxiety and the strenuous activity had made Moby sweat. Wisely he had packed a grocery bag with clean clothes, including his brand new Heart-A-Rama 2001 T-shirt. Moby removed his glasses, pulled off his drippy costume and reached blindly into his paper bag for his fresh shirt. Someone had opened the door at the back of the dressing room and the cool air hit his unconditioned, arthritic muscles and he tightened. With the garment above his head, he fought to shove his arms through first one hole and then the next.

Chip stepped into the room. He stopped. Watched. Shook his head. Moby was spinning and swearing "Sonofabitchsonofabitch" as he struggled to squeeze his head through the fly of a stretched out pair of underwear.

He grinned, thinking, I wonder if Moby swings both ways.

"Hey Moby, when you get your underwear on, how about coming over to my place for a quiet drink?'

Five years later . . .

Moby and Chip share an apartment. Chip works nine to five and Moby takes dance lessons.

Potential

by
Kevin Hansen

Marty Rashmister had been on this planet for a short six years. He lived in a quiet neighborhood on Manitowoc's north side near the Rahr West Art Museum. His house was a simple two story brick with a big front yard and an even bigger back yard. As an only child, Marty would have to admit his parents took great interest in his life. His dad was always there to encourage and take time to throw the ball around in the back yard. Marty's mom was always there, too. In fact, his mother was *ALWAYS* there. His mom saw something in him that he didn't. Marty's mom saw talent, or, as she put it "A certain twinkle that other little boys on the block don't have. Just no twinkle. Not like my Marty!" If there was one thing Marty knew for sure even at the age of six, it was that he didn't have talent, let alone "twinkle."

Most Saturday mornings in Marty's neighborhood, the boys got together for a game of kickball or they would ride their bikes down to the river to dig under rocks or rummage around in the woods. For Marty, Saturday morning meant getting in the car and taking a ride to the south side with his mom. A short drive to 15th and Hamilton Street. He absolutely dreaded the thought of walking up the steps to the second floor above Miss Carlisle's Curl Up and Dye House of Beauty. While his mother checked in for her weekly wash, set and style, Marty made the journey up the twenty-two steps to Mrs. Masapher's apartment. Catwoman. That's what everyone called her.

Mrs. Masapher had exactly seventeen cats of all colors and sizes. She knew each one by name and, after going to her apartment every Saturday for the past year, Marty was sure he knew every name, too. But the cats were not the reason Marty was coming to see the Catwoman. He was here to take piano lessons. Marty started taking lessons as a gift from his mom and dad for his fifth birthday. What Marty really wanted was a Tonka Fire Buster Action Set so he could play fireman like the real firefighters. But when he saw the looks of joy on his parents' faces when they showed him the piano they had wrapped up in the front sitting room, Marty didn't have the heart to look disappointed. He hugged them and told them how excited he was to take his first lesson. This enthusiasm didn't last long.

That first Saturday was much like every Saturday since. Marty would land at the top of the stairs and gently knock, while secretly hoping no one would answer. But it wouldn't take long and there would be a call from inside, "Come in, boy. I've been waiting for you. You're late. Our lessons start at eight and I expect my pupils to be on time." The truth was, Marty was always early. He believed that Mrs. Masapher could not really tell time. She said he was late every single Saturday since he started coming.

The piano lessons themselves were not all that bad. In fact, Marty was starting to get the hang of it. He wasn't exactly gifted; in fact, he really couldn't play a single song from his *Teaching Little Fingers to Play* book. But he could begin at middle C and work his was up to G and back down again without hesitation. He was surely getting the hang of it.

The worst part about coming to Mrs. Masapher was the smell of her apartment. Now you would think that with seventeen cats the smell would have been overpowering, but that wasn't it. The cats did give off a peculiar odor, but mixed with the fumes seeping up from the House of Beauty below, well, sometimes it made Marty's eyes water. At exactly 8 a.m. when he arrived it wasn't too bad, but by nine o'clock, after a few more perms had been started, well, Marty just about flew down those twenty-two steps after his lesson to escape the fumes.

Now, you might be wondering just why Marty's parents had come to believe that when it came to playing piano he had potential. Well, his potential surfaced shortly after his fourth birthday. One day, while Marty was playing in the garage, he began banging on an old toy piano that had been left over from the annual neighborhood rummage sale. Marty wasn't thinking about what he was doing—he was just having fun. But, by some strange coincidence, his playing sounded like something. It sounded so real that his mom came out to the garage to see who was playing. To her amazement, there was young Marty, working the keys like a pro. When his dad came home that evening, Mrs. Rashmister immediately sat him down in the living room.

"Now you just sit there and listen." And with that she escorted Marty into the room and sat him at the little piano which she had painstakingly placed in the exact center of the room. "Now play, Marty. Play for daddy."

Marty started banging on the piano trying to play like he had earlier, trying to make his mom happy. Klunk. Klunk. Klunk. Bing . . Bing . . .Bing . . .Those were the only sounds Marty could make. Those were the only sounds Marty could ever get that piano to make again. But he made them with style.

First his mom thought maybe he was just too nervous, or maybe he needed to be in the garage or maybe he needed a bigger piano. She tried everything but Klunk. Klunk. Klunk. Bing . . . Bing . . . Bing . . . That's all she got. And she didn't care; she really didn't because she knew that even though her son couldn't play the piano like before, she had heard him. She knew he had potential. "You just wait, Marty. You haven't begun to realize your full potential." With that came the piano lessons.

After Marty's usual Saturday morning lesson, they got back into the car and headed home. "Mom why are we going this way, are we stopping at the store before we go home?"

"No Marty, it's a surprise. You just sit tight."

A surprise! The last time Marty's mom gave him a surprise it meant spending Saturday mornings with the Catwoman. "Mom, really, where are we going?"

"Well, all right. I'll tell you. I can't believe I kept this to myself for so long anyway."

And with that she explained about the Ladies Auxiliary and how they were having a brunch this very day. Knowing her son's potential, Mrs. Rashmister volunteered him to be the entertainment.

He would play the piano for them. She had explained at the group's meeting two weeks earlier that, although only six, her son was enchanting. He had been studying for over a year and really was quite good. Marty's mom carried on about his debut, or as she called it, his "opening night," until he began to grow ill. His stomach rolled over and over.

"But Mom, I can hardly play the scales, what will I do? They'll want to hear a real song, and I can't do that."

"Now Marty, I know you've been working hard. Everyone will see that you have potential."

They arrived at the Auxiliary, Marty's mom proudly escorting him inside. With terror Marty sat down at the piano while his mom went to hang up their coats. More and more ladies filled the room and sat down. When everyone was in and settled, Marty's mom stepped to the piano and stood beside her son. "Ladies, it is my pleasure to introduce to you my 6 year old musical genius, Marty Rashmister." Marty did nothing. "Well, you can start, Marty," she whispered. "Everyone is here dear, so go ahead, play something."

"Here it goes," Marty thought to himself. "I'll play the best I can, but my best will be awful and maybe Mom will realize I don't have potential." And so Marty began to play. He played the scales up and he played the scales down. As he plunked them out, his mom looked on proudly. The other ladies just looked mortified. Their faces reminded Marty of the first time he went to the dentist to have a cavity filled. They were in pain. No doubt about it. But there his mom stood, proud as ever, with a bold look of encouragement on her face.

When he finished, the ladies were not sure what to do; there were muffled claps and a few murmurs. Soon the chatter picked up and everyone quickly began eating. Marty's mom told him it had gone well.

"Went well, Mom? How could anyone enjoy listening to me playing scales? Even Catwoman hates it, and she get paid to listen."

Mrs. Rashmister did not want to hear this. "You just need more practice. Remember, you have potential." The following Monday, Marty's mom added another night of piano lessons with

Mrs. Masapher. And then she went ahead and booked him to play at the Downtown Manitowoc Association's annual fashion extravaganza.

Five years later . . .

Marty is 11. His mom gave up on the lessons two years ago and sold the piano. About that same time, she caught a glimpse of Marty in the backyard, marching around with a stick and twirling it above his head. Now each Saturday morning Marty heads to the Children's Center of the Arts where he is enrolled in Toddy Dan's School of Tap and Baton. He still has potential.

Exit Lines

by
Emily M. Trask

The rows are empty now, the theater dark. Walking the aisles, the seats loom lonely for the moment and call out to me, one by one, for a body to embrace. Their velvet is crushed and softly worn on their backs and bottoms from the shifting weight caused by laughter and tears and the impatient smoker squirming until intermission. I assure them not to worry and without looking back, am on my way. It echoes—the space that my shoes click through and ricochets off the dreams and hopes of young, bright-eyed performers like myself. Leaving the hollow, quiet space, I disappear behind the curtain.

Eventually, you file in. Peering in pocket mirrors and toying with candy wrappers, not knowing me, I unknowing of you. Your whispers roll through the house like gray waves just before the storm breaks and I feel it. Costumed, warmed, and memorized, I pace. I breathe. I pace. I breathe in the dark backstage air that always seems thickest before my cue and I feel my stomach spin, loop, and fall. The "Five Minute" call seals my fate, and slowly I step into my character, feet first like footed pajamas, zipping up her sides, settling in. Then I walk around awhile, getting comfortable in another's skin—smiling how she would, sighing how she might. A feat so marvelous that, with your permission, I see the world through the tint of another's spectacles, a kind of second sight achieved in its greatest effort now, even if only for two hours. You see, in five minutes, she and I will step out into the puddle of light that spills onto the stage and laps over the edge, illuminating the first few rows of faces and fading slowly past the third. And just for an instant, I will hover there. And we will meet. We three. And you will know, and we shall become a trio for a time in a dance of exits and entrances, ups and downs—a theatrical waltz of people, persona, and person. Thebans and thespians.

I live out loud in those surrendering hours, those moments of suspension, the breaths of knowing something other than the now and ourselves. We gather on the fertile ground of belief.

So, I offer it all up. I give you the hours of rehearsals, the scratching memorization, the sighs of self-doubt, the tears of passion and need, the memories of nights long gone, glimmers of curtain calls taken, characters misinterpreted, pauses held too long, the realization that to fly, you often must fall, the dreams of things to come, the fear that they won't, the hope, the character, the story that is you and me. There now. I have laid it bare, willingly, readily, to be taken or declined. I wrap myself tightly in your hand with the program you roll and unroll in anticipation, and I ask you to step with me into the light here on stage where I almost understand and split with self-exposure as someone else.

Then. When it is over I go home, just like you do, run a warm bath like you might, peel the fake lashes from my lids, wash the makeup from my face, the smoke from my hair, and forget the lines momentarily until tomorrow's dusting. But tonight, I pass the steamy streaked mirror and pause. Wiping the glass with the back of my hand I make out the lips and the eyes and the ears of a rather plain girl. No Maggie the Cat or Lady Macbeth or Sally Bowles, just me. But . . . as I breathe in the heavy heated bathroom air, it spreads differently through my insides, like warm fingers reaching to something new Stepped from and unzipped, I realize the world is still tinted a slightly different shade than when this night began. *Her* shading lingers there behind my eyes and I see the world, myself, revised after having viewed it from another's gaze.

Admittedly, I am proud of it, of what it echoes here in *this* moment of suspension, under the too strong bathroom light where facades are known to melt. Not of the applause, which will ring and fade, or the smiles and handshakes which slip after a time, but for the twilight where we cohabitated for a moment . . . you, me, and the story in one shared breath. We are different for having known this and each other in this elusively intimate way. I am changed and better for it. It coats my interior even as this hot breath is exhaled and fogs the mirror of me again. This time I don't bother to wipe the perspiration from the glass. The only reflection which needs seeing is not that of a plain, selectively shy, redheaded girl, but this reflection on and retention of knowing something other than myself, and thereby myself more deeply, across the bridge of belief.

We each have our own opening nights in life. Some occur every day, others on a grander scale—times when we open our arms to what lies just beyond where we can see into the darkness, and we wait for our other, our audience, to file in and decide whether to dance or to deny. All we can do, standing isolated in the pool of light, is offer up our all in the chosen form, lay it bare on the boards, without knowing exactly why or where it's going when the story leaves us. This I strive to do readily, in each pursuit, and every morning. I open yet another "night" with this hymn of hope that these thoughts find a somewhat foggy future there with you, anticipating reaction and awaiting the next few steps of the dance that will surely be long remembered after the curtain falls.

Contributors

Bev Denor taught at Valders High School and freely admits that she got to play all day with highly creative writing and theater students. She also owns LaDeDa Books & Beans, where she is honored and humbled to rub elbows with the intelligentsia of Manitowoc County, many of whom are represented in this collection. In her spare time, she likes to putter behind the scenes in local theater productions, and regularly and passionately lies about her successful days on stage.

Rick Gerroll lives near Lake Michigan's shore in Manitowoc, Wisconsin, with wife Christine Kornely and Penelope, their English Bulldog. They work, love amateur theater, volunteer, hang with friends and enjoy the greater cosmic scheme of life.

Kevin Hansen spends his days as a marketing director, and for twenty-eight years has spent his nights working in amateur theater. His career began in 4th grade where he acted out a Greek myth for his classmates. He has no recall of the story but does remember wearing a kilt during the production (all Greeks wear kilts, right?). He fell off a ladder and from that moment his classmates knew just what type of underwear his mom bought for him. That incident pretty much shaped Kevin's entire life . . . just one fall after another with everyone looking up his skirt.

Gary Retzak was born in Milwaukee, Wisconsin and grew up in West Allis. He retired from the Navy's nuclear program in July of 1990. Gary's first theater experience occurred in third grade when he was asked to play the part of Saint Francis Assisi in a school play.

He stood center stage with a "deer in the headlights look" repeating each line the nun shouted from off stage. He was hooked! Gary would like readers to know that although Masquers did perform *The Sound of Music,* none of the incidents in his story actually took place. In fact, his story was inspired by a series of similar, but less spectacular events that took place at a local church.

Emily M. Trask attended school at the "family business"—the University of Wisconsin-Manitowoc, where her father teaches history, her mother advises students and where, for many years, her grandfather was a much-loved night watchman. Emily joined the local theater world when she was a senior in high school and has been going strong ever since. Even when not on stage, Emily could be caught performing periodically at a local bookstore where she sold books, served cappuccino and was the "Senior Vice President in Charge of Displays." Emily graduated from Grinnell College in Iowa and eventually went on to get her MFA at the Yale School of Drama. She has worked all across the country in from Broadway houses to Shakespeare tours ... but the lakeshore will always be home.

Kerry A. Trask is Professor Emeritus of History with the University of Wisconsin Colleges and taught at the UW-Manitowoc campus from 1972 until his retirement in 2008. He graduated from Hamline University in 1965 and received his M.A. and Ph.D. in history from the University of Minnesota in 1968 and 1971. A native of Canada, Trask has a particular interest in the early history of the Great Lakes region. He is the author of numerous articles and essays, as well as seven books, including his award winning works *Fire Within: A Civil War Narrative from Wisconsin* and *Black Hawk: The Battle for the Heart of America.* In 2008, based upon his lifetime achievements and contributions to education, Kerry was inducted into the Wisconsin Academy of Sciences, Arts, and Letters as a permanent fellow. Above all, he is especially proud to be the father of Emily and John-Peter, both of whom are creative people of unusual talent.

Brad Zimmermann is a native of Manitowoc. Involved in local theater since childhood, he has always enjoyed a little drama. Brad has been a part of many writing and acting endeavors all over the lakeshore, including local fund raiser Heart-A-Rama and filming a commercial for the Green Bay Packers. He credits his love of the daytime serials *One Life to Live* and *General Hospital*, an early obsession with author Phyllis A. Whitney, and his mother Suzanne for helping him develop a love of story, writing, and the magic of reading.